GATHER
DOWN WOMEN

GATHER
DOWN WOMEN

POEMS AND TRANSLATIONS BY MICHAEL GUSHUE

Souvenir
Spoon
Books

Washington, DC
2023

Please direct inquiries to:

Souvenir Spoon Books
921 Perry Place NE
Washington, DC 20017
info@spoonbooks.com

www.spoonbooks.com

Gushue, Michael —
Gather Down Women / by Michael Gushue — 1st ed.

Cover image: Detail of "Hecuba and Polyxena" by Merry-Joseph Blondel
(1781-1853).

Author photo courtesy of author.

Cover and interior design by Souvenir Spoon Books

REVISED SECOND EDITION
ISBN 979-8-9887951-0-0

ACKNOWLEDGEMENTS:

"Iphegeneia" appeared in *the americas review*.

OTHER BOOKS BY MICHAEL GUSHUE:

Sympathy for the Monster
The Judy Poems (with CL Bledsoe)
I Never Promised You A Sea Monkey
(with CL Bledsoe)
Pachinko Mouth
Conrad
Gather Down Women

For Susan.

GATHER DOWN WOMEN

...but it is a god who through all draws human souls
where he wills, making one dependent on another's power.

-Plato, Ion [536a]

Iphegeneia

Not knowing what to do, we asked the priest Calchis,
who proclaimed that I must slay one of my own flesh,
Iphegeneia, as a sacrifice to Artemis, who dwells
here...
                                        -Euripides: *Iphegeneia at Aulis*

You showed me how to loose bright thigh
meat from its column of bone, cut away
the thick tendon, wrap flesh in a caul
of fat. Walking back you let me carry
the shining blade in my small hand.
That night I watched as you rolled
a drop out of the two-handled cup,
let it fall to the ground, a black stain.

I dreamt a clearing of white sand, a bowl
edged in thorns and gorse. A hart leapt
from nowhere into that arena,
so close I felt its breath against
my cheek. Flames like curtains of sky
rippled around its body, up its neck
and motionless head, up past the antlers,
its eyes enormous, gold-black coins.

Today I found a sea urchin stranded
in a pool among the darkening rocks.
Its quills, ivory and royal purple,
waved like lances in the clear water.

I brought it to you among your ships.
Legs stained with salt, you held it as if
to listen, then threw it and turned to go.
My hand was wrapped in your glittering palm.

Xorós I

Gray

ache

pull down

speaking   empty out

go in fields

let the hard kernel

of word

deem

and the tongue of tongues

let it unname you

in its burning

Klytaimnestra

And there anger cannot be dislodged, terrible,
a treachery that governs the whole house
and always holds in mind: avenge your child.
                    -Aeschylus: *Agamemnon*

Not the trees, not the leaves or branches,
not the birds nesting in branches,
not the swallow, not the swifts, jays,
finches. Only the beak: hard, sharp.

Not the fruit heavy on the ends
of trees, not the apricots,
pomegranates, lemons or olives.
But the bitterness of olives.

Not the bushes, brambles or tangle,
not the shrubs, brush, not the berries,
not the fruit among leaves and cane.
Only the red stain, thorn's hold.

Not the vines, staked and shaped,
not the grapes, not the wine, sweetened,
or the cakes sponged in honey.
But the barb and the venom.

Not the crafts, the ornaments or gold,
not the iron stays and hinges.
Only the bitterness of iron,
iron's unbending heart.

Not seeds or life, and not summer,
not the season's pull, not birth, not
children. But this: hard, hold, unbending—
this:

iron

venom

beak

strike

Hekabe

I turned my face to the great dying river
and a dry wind entered me. I am
a woman violated by an angry god.
Clouds bloomed beneath my skin,
I don't remember even yesterday
where I walked or who I spoke to—

I set my head against hard earth,
The things there do not hear,
but deep inside were stirring,
beetles are dragging themselves
across the broken ground.

My bare feet burn in this dry season
and the hills burn white like flares.
I stop a stranger and—
my heart hidden in its walnut shell—
my heart of milkweed, of thorn—
whisper my name as he seizes me.

I am scattered by wind, a husk
split in its own unwinding chamber.
Where the wind and parched earth meet—
you cannot touch me without bleeding.

Every day I must wash the hair
on this body a thousand times,
my body a wound that must be cleansed.
At night I face the great dying mirror—

the moon—old thief, old trespasser—
his long finger a bone of light—
steals another silver coin
from the sea's reluctant mouth.

Kassandra

Kassandra: Am I false prophet, some beggar spewing nonsense?
Swear here that I speak the ancient sins of this house.

Chorus: How can words—even sworn in honor—sooth you?
And yet we are amazed: though born across the sea,
your strange tongue shows what lies hidden, as if you
had stood here with us...

- Aeschylus: *Agamemnon*

Shipdeck at noon. Where, King, is your
shadow? Beneath you: larval, hidden.
Your shadow is also a tide, it pulls
until flesh aches to leave bone.

I dreamt your horses pulled riders
onto the sand, great necks twisting,
reaching for thigh and arm—tearing.
Today, your oars cut the dark water
until the sea is all one wound.

I dreamt you in your robes, sodden,
too heavy to move. They pull you down.
A flood rushes over the wide steps
of your courtyard, the black sea rolls
my tangled body stung by the waves.

At noon your shadow hides under you—
the tide's muscled knot—the sea's torso—
pushing it back and forth: now—not now—
now—and there is a god in my throat.

Elektra

The torches flare all around us at night.
Inside their heat are words with no sound,
but bright. Let them sear my tongue.

Brother, I've walked this dry road without
sandals, left footprints wet with blood.
I have seen a god—a snake—strike at stones,
seen them bleed, your name in their fault.

Hold this bowl of riverwater and sand, stir it
and watch. Water glitters as it clears.
Go back to the city, our home, the threshold

and leave your name behind, let
the spreading flames bind you—take
up his robes, stained, stiffened, black.
Break the staff. Enter her bedchamber.

Orestes/Eumenides

Look: our earth's womb, foul
with the reeking blood violating it.
                    - Aeschylus: *The Eumenides*

Chlorine sky—ahead a mud field,
stones breaching earth: black flukes, burnt root,
the cries of birth—all heat and flux.
Ruddy slick smears up my/his calves and
my/his ankle snaps outward in the wet muck.

A fissure opens, abdomen's spill,
wet jewels pour out, a loop of bracelets,
the air arches and falls as hours wade
through the darkness. When skin is broken,
the fire of years cracks the glaze.

A winter's wind shreds the sea in March
and on the scree beach, my/his father's bones wash up,
frayed like rope. Now salt and drift, they splinter
on oxblood rocks, plunge from a precipice,
a blinding place, blazing sun proceeding.

I/he am/is still found in that mouth.
Speech burns off moisture, the smell of the marsh.
There's the house, always smaller than memory,
wavering. Come closer where the door's ajar:
The room opens, and swallows me/him.

Xorós II

Heave   earth

from your breath

turn words

hollow clay

water

and pour out

down

where tongue

marries throat—

let root light.

Ismene

Do not fear for me.
Look to correct your
own evil destiny.
                    -Sophocles: *Antigone*

Oh sister, take me away from this river;
the cicadas are as loud as blood.
They roost like crows in the laurel, their
green armor is a spearpoint of anger.

Tonight every eye is against us,
the city's hard cry surging up
with a crest rattling like bronze,
rising through streets to our window.

Sister, the bones of my thighs cry out,
and this cradle of bone fills with tears,
and this black stone called my heart,
where can I hide it? It has no home.

Oh let us flee and let wasps
eat our lives of bruised fruit.
Let the dry mountains embrace us—
the wind hot, a jackal of salt.

Can't you still hear the bellowing?
As if the sky's throat were being cut
or in the square, slaughtering bull after bull,
until their hands disappear in the steam.

Medeia

This anger arising from lover and loved joined
in war with each other: terrible, incurable.
                    - Euripides: Chorus in *Medea*

What happened, husband, to our road?
You stagger, a bear drunk on spoiled fruit—
gold wine, honeyed squab at your table—
the swing of your eyes seeking
a gleam of morsel hung out of reach.

I remember your sleek hair shining as
you stepped down from your ship's prow.
I could smell the salt air on you, clean
and sweet as you walked past me, glanced
towards me, your eyes olive and searching.

It is time you found the world's heart
is Serpent: it coils and coils on itself.
You can see it in the fat hide of Ocean,
the mouths of rivers, the way planets
twist their tetherless paths each night.

You can see it, the knot, the skein inside me,
a black nest turning on itself.
The earth will swarm over you, curl
into your chest like a wasp, wait there,
its head of bronze glinting and fierce.

Husband, ask: where are they, your children?
Two jars, necks cracked, spill and spill
as a clot of red silk unravels across
my wet hands. Ask—your mouth
slack—whose feast is this, about to start?

Alkheistis

But I reap an even greater profit
from those who die young.
      - Euripides: *Alcestis*

At our last feast I lay next to you
and held in my hand a wedge of fig,
its juice clung to my palm
as I offered it to you, full of seed,
sweet pulp—the whole room
swooned in its sugar.

Midnight, I stood beneath black
pines, waiting, half in shadow
and my body—half flesh, half shade—
was a fruit melting into the ground.

Out on the marsh at dusk I saw
a black swan descend to the water,
the high grass, and rear up as it landed,
its great wings spread like split halves
of night's faceless sky. Its red bill
flared in the light at day's end.

Galateia

I awoke sunk beneath
a pool of milk, a doll
nestled in algae and clay.

The walls of the room
were streaked red and
burnished, and my tears

fell in shards like sentences,
like the water clock draining
in your house: you gave me

my sex and my hands.
Through the courtyard
a light shone and showed

the blue tiles of the larger
house containing yours.
I was ready to leave,

but you gave me a small
marble lozenge to swallow
as I stared at the emptying sleeves—

Ekho

"One day the nymph Eckho saw him,
Narkissos, driving frightened deer into his nets—
she who cannot be silent when others have spoken,
and cannot speak for herself."
-Ovid: Metamorphoses

A god took its bright spear, thrust
through the gate of my mouth,
the point twisted around, around.

My voice was chaff taken by wind,
all the words in me headless birds
falling like stones from a black sky.

How I ache for silence, to curl
into its dark hollow, its small nest,
a woodthrush exhausted by song.

Beautiful hunter, I saw you climbing
white Kithairon, its limestone face
tall as a wave where you shone forth.

Hunter, your words push into me.
My splintering tongue bursts
in the red mirror of my throat.

Ariadne

The sea is torn flint
and strikes the rocks
where my voice echoes
without a body
into crevices
littered with seadrift.
The faint sound
of waves and wind
erodes—a swarm of wasps—
my hard unspoken knot.

I lay down under
the ocean's resinous eye—
olive-colored and
streaked with departure,
and cannot fill the empty,
this bowl of days.

My birth is exile:
I swallow stones salted
with the sweat of horses.
Dark hooves pound the coast
and I cry out: pull in—
pull in, pull in
the thallasic reins,
wrench the black leather
from my grip,
clot my white throat
with vermilion and clay.

If I shed that heat,
uproot my womb like a sapling,
if the sound of bronze
breaks the bones of my mouth,

if my grief dries to a thistle
of blood, if I fold my cries
beneath the wings of petrels—

but the sea is a broken stone,
a fragment of sun, a pebble
lodged behind my tongue:
in a basin of stone,
at the sea's fluent gate,
spun and swirled about,
until nothing is left.

Philomena

Last night I bathed in the blood of oranges,
the peel ruptured, the flesh black—
the moonlight was searing and acid.

I felt mirrors and fish leap in my thighs,
the pebble of my sex, the rose-milk
of my belly, through the flute of my spine.

I was drowning in red, swallowed—
my back arched over fields of sulfur,
a kestrel consumed in an agate fire.

I was burning—my blood was burning
through me, and a thousand moths
flamed against my throat,

against my thighs, the soles of my feet,
and my voice—my soundless voice—waking—
a thousand moths dying inside my voice.

Nymphai Mysiai

...Hylas, Thiodamus' son, Hercules' love,
was sent to draw water where the Mysian Naiads
—seeing his beauty—seized and ravished him.
              -Apollodorus: *Library and Epitome*

Come drink from our river of flutes—
emeralds will not soothe you.
Dive into this ocean our forest:
green orchids wave in jealousy,
drops of opal covet your eyes,
your body inked by shadow.

Your hands drink water abandoned
by trees. Let our words circle your waist
like the seeds of pomegranates.
Let your mouth drown against our lips,
beneath the waves of our leaves,

and let our kisses feather you,
our tongues of water in the forest's
green throat. We'll sing in your hair,
cormorants of green copper.
Is not your blood the plumage of seas?
Is not your skin embossed by Ocean?

And when the rose pearl of sex rises
through the banyan of our limbs, when

our forest winds through you
in vines of rain—when this river
swells—a green fountain pulsing—
your body will braid and braid us
with your white verb—in the rhythm,
in the jade tide of our wombs.

Xorós III

Untongued

arms thinned

to wheatstraw—

throat whittled

with ash

layer

down

it all:

burnt chaff

to the black earth.

Ostrakon

"But now stop; raise your lament no further.
All that has happened is redeemed in this end."
                    -Sophocles, *Oedipus at Colonus*

When the day begins the thin light
is straw-colored and confuses our path,
and the sand is cold beneath my feet.

Here at the wrackline I pick through
charred pieces tangled in rope and kelp
now cool to the touch. So much

could rise up and devour us: glass, rust,
the ragged edges of history, of tribe.
Anger is a tide, it seizes and holds our hearts.

Sister, look, here are green shreds of net,
the drowned bramble of the sea:
shell, flint, quartz, soothed into shape by water.

Over here are shrouded forms, hollow and bruised—
and here are the ones who fell, or foundered,
or were carried away far from shore.

Sister, what shall we call what is left for us?
Call it our destroyed—our indestructible—world.
And this morning, we must go together

and live in each other's brokenness.
Here, lift up our defiled father, wrap his cloak
around him. Hold him up. Take him home.

Xorós IV

Reach   speak

let mouth gather its ashword

of saying

empty   grass

hard   ground

let   the earth

speak

from your wound

YES   BE

ALL   FLAME

NOTES

"Gather Down Women" is a literal translation of Gynaikon Katalogos, an early epic poem (roughly 700 BC, about the same time as Homer) attributed to Hesiod; also known as Ehoiai from the formula phrase "e hoie" ("Or such a woman as").

Iphegeneia (Iphegenia) was the daughter of Agamemnon and Klytaimnestra. Agamemnon, as head of the Achaeans, sacrificed her to Artemis on the island of Aulis so the becalmed Achaean fleet could sail to Troy and start the Trojan War. Agamemnon's killing her was one of the reasons his wife Clytemnestra plotted to murder him and usurp the throne when he returned home to Achaea (mainland Greece) after the war. Iphegenia is speaking on the day of her death, unaware it is immanent.

Xorós is from the Greek word "xorós" meaning to chant oracles or deliver them in verse.

Klytaimnestra (Clytemnestra) was Agamemnon's wife. She nursed her hatred for him—for murdering Iphegenia—during the ten years he was away and plotted to kill him. After his return, she attacked and slaughtered him as he taking a bath and then killed his concubine, Kassandra. Clytemnestra is speaking just before the return of the fleet.

Hekabe (Hecuba) was King Priam's (of Troy) wife. She was enslaved by the Achaeans after the fall of Troy, went mad on seeing the corpses of her children Polydorus and Polyxena and killed herself by throwing herself in the Hellespont. She is speaking after she has gone mad.

Kassandra (Cassandra) was Agememnon's concubine/slave after the fall of Troy. She had the gift of prophecy but was cursed with the condition that no one would believe her prophecies (which were all true). She is speaking on Agamemnon's ship before reaching Achaea.

Elektra (Electra) was Agamemnon's daughter. She is speaking in exile, urging Orestes to avenge his father's death.

Orestes was Agamemnon's son. He avenged his father's death by killing his mother Klytaimnestra and her lover, and as a result was pursued by the Furies (the Erinyes or Eumenides) for committing matricide.

Eumenides were chthonic female deities of punishment and vengeance. They were called Eumenides ("Kindly Ones") as a euphemism for their real name, Erinys ("Furies"). There were three Furies: Alecto ("unceasing"), Megaera ("grudging"), and Tisiphone ("avenging murder"). Their eyes drip blood, they have snakes for hair and are more terrible to look upon than gorgons or harpies. Both Orestes and the Eumenides are speaking in unison as Orestes approaches the palace where his mother is, the Eumenides in an augmented fourth above Orestes voice.

Ismene was one of Oedipus' daughters. She tried to dissuade Antigone (his other daughter) from burying her slain brothers, an act for which Antigone would be put to death. Ismene is speaking to Antigone the night before Antigone goes out of the city gates and buries them.

Medeia (Medea) helped Jason steal the Golden Fleece. She was a sorceress, priestess and barbarian from Colchis, the end of the world. Jason married her, had two sons by her and then abandoned her to make a politically advantageous marriage to the king of Corinth's daughter. Medeia killed Jason's bride and her own two sons. She fled in a chariot pulled by two winged dragons. Medea is speaking the night before committing these deeds.

Alkheistis (Alcestis) was the wife of King Admetus. Apollo granted Admetus the favor of being able to have someone die in his place. When he found out he was going to die very soon (and relatively young) he looked for someone to take his place. Everyone refused to die in his place, including (especially) his very old parents. But his wife Alcestis agreed to take his place. Alcestis is speaking on the evening before her death.

Galatea was a statue carved by Pygmalion, so perfect it came to life. She is speaking as she transforms from marble to flesh in his studio.

Ekho (Echo) was an Oread on Mount_Kithairon. After she distracted Hera as Zeus lay with other mountain nymphs. She was punished by having her voice taken away, only able to repeat the last words spoken to her. She is speaking after seeing and hearing Narkissos (Narcissus).

Ariadne was the daughter of King Minos of Crete. She helped Theseus defeat the Minotaur and escape the labyrinth where the Minotaur was housed. Theseus took her with him when escaping Crete but abandoned her on the island of Naxos. Ariadne is speaking sometime after being abandoned on the otherwise uninhabited island.

Philomena was a young girl raped by her brother-in-law, Tereus. He cut out her tongue to keep her from revealing what had happened, but she wove a tapestry telling the story. The gods turned her into a nightingale. She is speaking after being raped and mutilated.

Nymphai Mysiai (Mysian Nymphs) were Naiads (fresh water semi-deities). They fell in love with Hylas, Hercules' young male lover, because of his beauty and drowned him. The Naiads are speaking to Hylas.

An **ostrakon** is a fragment of shattered pottery used as a ballot in Athens when there was a council vote to send someone into exile. The word "ostracize" comes from this. In the poem a young Antigone is speaking to Ismene. They were their father's caretaker after he blinded himself and was sent into exile from Thebes. She is speaking as they walk a shoreline, headed towards Kolonus where Oedipus meets his end.

The last four words of this book derive from this story found in the Greek text *Apophthegmata Patrum*:

Abba Lot went to see Abba Joseph and said to him, *"Abba as far as I can I say my little office, I fast a little, I pray and meditate, I live in peace and as far as I can, I purify my thoughts. What else can I do?"* Then the old man stood up and stretched his hands towards heaven. His fingers became like ten lamps of fire and he said, *"If you will, you can become all flame."*

Michael Gushue is co-curator of the poetry incubator Poetry Mutual, and publishes the works of others through 81Names Press, Beothuk Books, Editorial Pretzelcoatl, and the forthcoming reprint series Fenix Books. He co-curated the Poetry at the Watergate, Capitol Hill Reading Series, and the Brookland Poetry Series. His other books include *Sympathy for the Monster*, *Pachinko Mouth, Conrad*, and, in collaboration with CL Bledsoe, *I Never Promised You A Sea Monkey* and *The Judy Poems*. He makes his home in the Brookland neighborhood of Washington, DC.

Washington, DC

About Souvenir Spoon Books

Since 2011, we've been dedicated to publishing collections of poetry that catch our eye. Small or large, full or chap, the size isn't as important as much as the delight the work inspires in us to share it with a wider audience. While not the *only* reason to publish books, we certainly believe it's one of the best ones. The micro-press is named after the antique spoons collected by its founder – little works of art that "speak" with a deep sense of place and record history and image through enormous dedication and craftsmanship: a fitting symbol for the books of poetry we publish. Souvenir Spoon Books previously published Michael Gushue's *Conrad*.

Enjoy and thanks for supporting good contemporary poetry!

www.spoonbooks.com

www.ingramcontent.com/pod-product-compliance
Lightning Source LLC
Chambersburg PA
CBHW061503170626
46811CB00004B/1600